LASSIE COME-HOME

AN ADAPTATION OF ERIC KNIGHT'S CLASSIC STORY

WRITTEN BY SUSAN HILL

ILLUSTRATED BY OLGA & ALEKSEY IVANOV

HENRY HOLT AND COMPANY · NEW YORK

TO OUR MOTHERS
—O. I. & A. I.

Henry Holt and Company, LLC
Publishers since 1866
175 Fifth Avenue
New York, New York 10010
mackids.com

Library of Congress Cataloging-in-Publication Data
Hill, Susan, 1965–
Lassie come-home : an adaptation of Eric Knight's classic story / Susan Hill ; illustrated by Aleksey & Olga Ivanov.
pages   cm
Summary: After losing his job, Joe's father has no choice but to sell Joe's beloved collie,
Lassie, to a wealthy duke, but when the duke takes her to the far north of Scotland,
Lassie undertakes a 1,000-mile journey to be reunited with her boy.
ISBN 978-1-62779-294-3 (hardback)
[1. Dogs—Fiction. 2. Yorkshire (England)—Fiction. 3. England—Fiction.] I. Ivanov, A. (Aleksey), illustrator.
II. Ivanov, O. (Olga), illustrator. III. Knight, Eric, 1897–1943. Lassie come-home. IV. Title.
PZ7.H5574Las 2015   [E]—dc23   2014045705

Henry Holt books may be purchased for business or promotional use.
For information on bulk purchases, please contact the Macmillan Corporate and Premium Sales Department
at (800) 221-7945 x5442 or by e-mail at specialmarkets@macmillan.com.

First Edition—2015 / Designed by April Ward
The artists used pencil and watercolor on paper to create the illustrations for this book.

Printed in China by RR Donnelley Asia Printing Solutions Ltd., Dongguan City, Guangdong Province

1 3 5 7 9 10 8 6 4 2

Lassie! You've come home!" Joe threw his arms around the sable collie.

Never had a boy and a dog loved each other more. But Lassie belonged to the Duke of Rudling now. When the coal mine shut down and Father was out of work, Father had no choice but to sell her.

Yet Lassie had run back to Joe again to meet him after school the way she always did.

"We *must* keep her, now she's come home again,"
Joe said to Mother and Father. "Not once but twice
she's got away from Mr. Hynes!" Hynes was the Duke's
kennelman; he didn't have a tender touch for any dog.

Mother spoke sharply. "We can't afford to feed
ourselves, let alone a dog. There's no work coming,
hard as Father tries."

"We could hide her," Joe said, "and the Duke would never know!"

Father shook his head. "When a fellow doesn't have much, Joe," he said, "honesty's about all he does have."

Joe went with Father to return Lassie to the
Duke's kennel. The Duke's granddaughter, Priscilla,
was there. Joe couldn't bear for anyone to see him cry.
He squeezed his eyes shut and said to Lassie, "Stay, girl,
and never, never come home to us. We don't want you
anymore." His voice was loud and gruff, to wall up the
tears behind his words.

In the next days, Joe hoped Lassie would escape once more and meet him after school as she always had done. But Lassie did not come again.

"The Duke took the dog to his place in Scotland," Father said. "Four hundred miles hard by the road, and who knows how many more miles for a dog to make her way." Father briefly clasped Joe's shoulder. "It's a long way, Joe," he said.

Joe thought of the wild miles that separated him from Lassie, the moors and wide rivers and lochs. "Then it's true," he said. "Lassie will never come home again."

In the Highlands of Scotland, Lassie knew the chain
around her neck, the iron bars of her cage, and the howling
of the wind. And she knew, each day, around the time her
food was set before her, that she belonged somewhere else.

Priscilla remembered the boy who'd hidden his tears and
gruffly bid the dog stay. Was he why the dog whimpered
so and pulled at the chain that bound her?

One day, Lassie slipped from Mr. Hynes's grasp.
Priscilla saw the dog bounding toward her, and she
opened the gate. Lassie ran through and away, never
slowing, never looking back.

"Good-bye, Lassie," Priscilla said softly. "Good luck."

It would be a long road for a dog with no guide.

Lassie bounded south
over heather and moor,
path and plowland . . .

across river and stream,
brook and brae,

and loch.

She met foe

and friend . . .

and always she kept to the way ahead.

So passed the miles, days, months, and seasons,

until at last, at last, came the village . . .

the street,

the schoolyard,

the gate,

and the boy.

Joe saw the dog lying at the gate. She could not lift her head; she could not wag her torn, ragged tail. But she whined weakly, happily, when Joe took up Lassie in his arms.

Joe ran like thunder down the road to the cottage.

"Mother! Lassie's come home! She's come home!"

Many days passed. Joe didn't know whether
Lassie would live or die. Then came the day Lassie
thumped her tail on the floor where she lay. And
then came the day she rose to her feet to lap from
a bowl of milk.

And then came another day, when the Duke of
Rudling arrived to take back what he'd paid for in
shillings and pounds.

But the Duke surprised them all.

"I couldn't take that dog," said the Duke. "Not when I saw the scarred pads of her feet. I thought of the miles she'd traveled from Scotland to Yorkshire—a thousand miles for a dog across the country—all to get home to her boy."

"Then you let Joe keep her?" Priscilla asked.

"Nonsense! I hired the boy's father. A fine kennelman, he is, and with the man and his kin, I gain the dog!"

Joe ruffled Lassie's sable coat, brushed soft and clean and fine as a Yorkshire summer, and Lassie lifted her head to him as if to say, *Here I am. Here I am, come home.*